TAKE CARE

Madelyn Rosenberg

pictures by
Giuliana Gregori

Albert Whitman & Company
Chicago, Illinois

Take care of the world

Of the mountains and trees

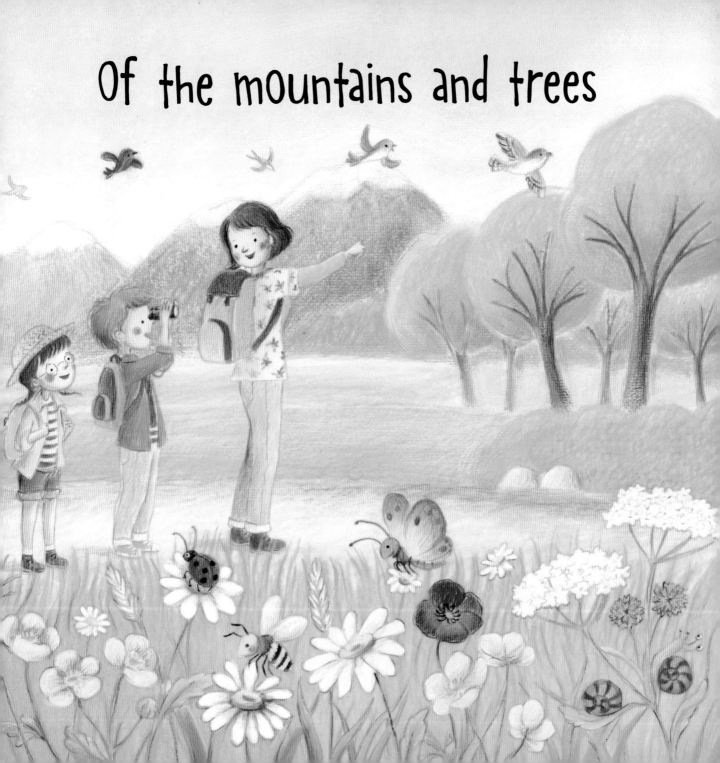

Tend to the world

All the bumbles and bees

Color the world

With greens and with blues

Heal up the world

With the words that you choose

Light up the world

Travel the world

All the up and down miles

Sail through the world

Let the wind steer you right

Wish with the world

On a dark, starry night

Reach out to the world

To the big and the small

Share the wide world

It belongs to us all.

For Kase and Ramona—MR

In memory of my dearest mother—GG

Library of Congress Cataloging-in-Publication data is on file with the publisher.

Text copyright © 2018 by Madelyn Rosenberg
Pictures copyright © 2018 by Albert Whitman & Company
Pictures by Giuliana Gregori
Published in 2018 by Albert Whitman & Company
ISBN 978-0-8075-7732-5

Printed in China
10 9 8 7 6 5 4 3 2 1 LP 22 21 20 19 18 17

Design by Jordan Kost

For more information about Albert Whitman & Company,
visit our website at www.albertwhitman.com.